Katharine Tynan

The Wind in the Trees

A Book of Country Verse

Katharine Tynan

The Wind in the Trees
A Book of Country Verse

ISBN/EAN: 9783337227869

Printed in Europe, USA, Canada, Australia, Japan

Cover: Foto ©Andreas Hilbeck / pixelio.de

More available books at **www.hansebooks.com**

THE WIND
IN THE TREES

A BOOK OF

COUNTRY VERSE BY

KATHARINE TYNAN

(MRS. HINKSON)

LONDON
GRANT RICHARDS
9 Henrietta Street
1898

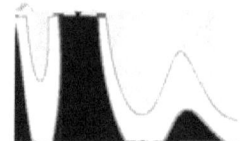

To ALICE MEYNELL

sweeter than summer

CONTENTS

vii

CONTENTS

CONTENTS

TURN O' THE YEAR

This is the time when bit by bit
The days begin to lengthen sweet,
And every minute gained is joy—
And love stirs in the heart of a boy.

This is the time the sun, of late
Content to lie abed till eight,
Lifts up betimes his sleepy head—
And love stirs in the heart of a maid.

This is the time we dock the night
Of a whole hour of candlelight;
When song of linnet and thrush is heard—
And love stirs in the heart of a bird.

A   I

TURN O' THE YEAR

This is the time when sword-blades green,
With gold and purple damascene,
Pierce the brown crocus-bed a-row—
And love stirs in a heart I know.

ST. VALENTIN

THE West wind blew so sweet and cold,
  The country wind and dear,
From fields and woods and gardens old
  In the morning of the year.
The pleasant sparrows, rooks, and daws
  Drank up that wind like wine,
And hailed the day with loud applause
  And chatterings gay and fine,
            Because
  It was St. Valentine.

The larks were fleeting near the earth,
  And fluttering high and low;
The blackbird joined his golden mirth
  To Spring's triumphal show.

3

ST. VALENTINE

The thrush was gathering twigs and straws
    All day in that sweet shine,
And feathers from the briars and haws
    Some bed of love to line,
          Because
    It was St. Valentine.

DAFFODIL

Who passes down the wintry street?
       Hey, ho, daffodil!
A sudden flame of gold and sweet.

With sword of emerald girt so meet,
And golden gay from head to feet.

How are you here this wintry day?
       Hey, ho, daffodil!
Your radiant fellows yet delay.

No windflower dances scarlet gay,
Nor crocus-flame lights up the way.

5

DAFFODIL

What land of cloth o' gold and green,
   Hey, ho, daffodil !
Cloth o' gold with the green between,

Was that you left but yestere'en
To light a gloomy world and mean ?

King trumpeter to Flora queen,
   Hey, ho, daffodil !
Blow, and the golden jousts begin.

PINK ALMOND

So delicate, so airy,
The almond on the tree,
Pink stars that some good fairy
Has made for you and me.

A little cloud of roses,
All in a world of gray,
The almond-flower uncloses
Upon the wild March day.

A mist of roses blowing
The way of fog and sleet,
A dust of roses showing
For gray dust in the street.

7

PINK ALMOND

Pink snow upon the branches,
  Pink snowflakes falling down
In rosy avalanches
  Upon the dreary town.

A rain, a shower of roses,
  All in a roseless day;
The almond-tree uncloses
  Her roses on the gray.

CUCKOO'S WAY

Domestic birds to build the nest
    May toil through April month and May,
And watch beside a brooding breast ;
    But that's not Master Cuckoo's way

He and his mistress, blithe as June,
    Roam like a gypsy pair at play,
Grow gold and brown in sun and moon,
    For that is still the Cuckoo's way.

'Out on your nurseries !' cries his wife ;
    'One egg's enough for me to lay,
To plague the sober sparrow's life ' ;
    For that is Mistress Cuckoo's way.

9

She cares not for the helpless brood
   Whom her bold son evicts one day,
Nor yellow beaks agape for food ;
   Oh, that's not Mistress Cuckoo's way !

This faithless pair, to duty blind,
   Reproach still answering, blithe and gay,
Free lovers in the sun and wind,
   For that is glad, the Cuckoo's way.

Despite the moral saws you bring,
   'Cuckoo!' 's their one excuse to say,
Flung from the golden throat of spring,
   For that is sweet, the Cuckoo's way.

CHESTNUT IN APRIL

The chestnut is a candlestick
Of arching clusters, rosy and thick,
And branches branching wide and high
Toward the smiling sky.

Closed are the sweet-lip buds that hide
A flame of mother-o'-pearl inside.
Open, open, O rosy mouth !
The wind is from the south.

O wind, from Spring's own country blow,
Till all the candles lit a-row,
And all the candles lit a-ring,
Make Christmas trees for Spring.

11

CHESTNUT IN APRIL

The little candle-cups are made
Of silver, rosy pearl, and jade.
Each cup shall hold its light aloft,
Moon-pale in wood and croft.

Not finer in the sky above
The heavenly candlestick, whereof
The candles are the stars that keep
Light while the sun 's asleep.

O chestnut, light your million lamps
In fairy camps, in dew and damps,
And draw the moths at eve to play
Around their glimmering ray.

O chestnut, light your lamps all pale,
The nights are for the nightingale.
Amid your lamps Love's bower is made:
Love's litanies are prayed.

CHESTNUT IN APRIL

Too soon, too soon on hill and lawn,
Like him who quenches lamps at dawn,
Shall one blow out your lights and leave
The woods to dusky eve.

EASTER

Bring flowers to strew His way,
Yea, sing, make holiday;
Bid young lambs leap,
And earth laugh after sleep.

For now He cometh forth
Winter flies to the north,
Folds wings and cries
Amid the bergs and ice.

Bring no sad palms like those
That led Him to His foes,
Bring windflower, daffodil,
From many a vernal hill.

14

EASTER

Let there be nought but bloom
To light Him from the tomb
Who late hath slain
Death, and his glory ta'en.

Yea, Death, great Death is dead,
And Life reigns in his stead;
Cometh the Athlete
New from dead Death's defeat.

Cometh the Wrestler,
But Death he makes no stir,
Utterly spent and done,
And all his kingdom gone.

Bring flowers, make holiday,
In His triumphal way.
Salve ye with kisses
His hurts that make your blisses.

EASTER

Bring flowers, make holiday,

For His triumphal way:

Yea, fling before Him

Hearts of men that adore Him.

GREEN SPRING

As I walked out on May-day E'en,
The land was like a girl in green,
With bloom of pear and bloom of plum,
Like lilies new in bloom.

When I walked out the First o' May,
The land a living emerald lay;
Soft flames of green the trees stood up
Out of an emerald cup.

O rain that raineth every day,
And clothes the sward and clothes the spray
With dew of diamond, veil of green,
And silver set between!

GREEN SPRING

O rain that rained the whole year through,
I heard the green things praising you,
The sap was flowing fast as rain
In many an emerald vein.

Are some will choose the golden Spring
With golden sky and golden wing,
And golden swallows faring home
Across the golden foam.

I praise the green Spring, silver and green,
Her skies that wash the grey world clean,
Then clothe it in the grass-green silk
With wimple white as milk.

LAMBS

He sleeps as a lamb sleeps,
  Beside his mother.
Somewhere in yon blue deeps
  His tender brother
Sleeps like a lamb and leaps.

He feeds as a lamb might,
  Beside his mother.
Somewhere in fields of light
  A lamb, his brother,
Feeds, and is clothed in white.

LARKS

ALL day in exquisite air
The song clomb an invisible stair,
Flight on flight, story on story,
Into the dazzling glory.

There was no bird, only a singing,
Up in the glory, climbing and ringing,
Like a small golden cloud at even,
Trembling 'twixt earth and heaven.

I saw no staircase winding, winding,
Up in the dazzle, sapphire and blinding,
Yet round by round, in exquisite air,
The song went up the stair.

LEAVES

Myriads and myriads plumed their glistening
    wings,
As fine as any bird that soars and sings,
As bright as fireflies or the dragon-flies,
Or birds of paradise.

Myriads and myriads waved their sheeny fans,
Soft as the dove's breast, or the pelican's;
And some were gold, and some were green, and
    some
Pink-lipped, like apple-bloom.

A low wind tossed the plumage all one way,
Rippled the gold feathers, and green and gray,—
A low wind that in moving sang one song
All day and all night long.

LEAVES

Sweet honey in the leafage, and cool dew,
A roof of stars, a tent of gold and blue ;
Silence and sound at once, and dim green light,
To turn the gold day night.

Some trees hung lanterns out, and some had stars,
Silver as Hesper, and rose-red as Mars ;
A low wind flung the lanterns low and high,—
A low wind like a sigh.

Myriads and myriads, more in number than
The sea's sands, or its drops of water wan,
Sang one Name in the rapture that is May ;
With faces turned one way.

CHANTICLEER

Of all the birds from East to West,
　　That tuneful are and dear,
I love that farmyard bird the best,
　　They call him Chanticleer.

Gold plume and copper plume,
　　Comb of scarlet gay ;
'Tis he that scatters night and gloom,
　　And whistles back the day !

He is the sun's brave herald
　　That, ringing his blithe horn,
Calls round a world dew-pearled
　　The heavenly airs of morn.

CHANTICLEER

O clear gold, shrill and bold,
  He calls through creeping mist
The mountains from the night and cold
  To rose and amethyst.

He sets the birds to singing,
  And calls the flowers to rise ;
The morning cometh, bringing
  Sweet sleep to heavy eyes.

Gold plume and silver plume,
  Comb of coral gay ;
'Tis he packs off the night and gloom,
  And summons home the day !

Black fear he sends it flying,
  Black care he drives afar ;
And creeping shadows sighing
  Before the morning star.

('Tis O, and woe, the lone ghost
  That glides before his call,
And huddles in its grave, so lost,
  Below the churchyard wall!)

The birds of all the forest
  Have dear and pleasant cheer,
But yet I hold the rarest
  The farmyard Chanticleer.

Red cock **or** *black* **cock,**
  Gold cock or white,
The flower of all the feathered flock,
  He whistles back the light !

THE GARDENER

For the light heart or heavy heart
Medicine.   Set thou a time apart,
And to thy garden thee betake
With hoe and spade and pot and rake.

Mark thou thy garden,—and not spare
Thyself as honest labourer.
Break thou the earth and turn withal,
So the live airs thereon shall fall.

Then set thy little seeds in rows,
With the kind earth for swaddling-clothes.

THE GARDENER

And these shall presently awake,
And into life and praise shall break.

Hoe, thin, and water then, that these
May spread their growing limbs at ease ;
And prune the vaulting boughs lest they
Should dwindle for the warmth of day.

Soon shall the sweet Spring trumpets ring,
And all the world sing songs for Spring :
Then from the wormy bed shall rise
Creatures that wear the peacock's eyes.

No man shall childless go who hath
Raised these sweet babies out of death.
O peachy cheeks and goldilocks,
And maids in rose and scarlet frocks !

THE GARDENER

Here shall resort the butterfly,
The birds set up their loves hereby.
The mealy-mouthed bee shall come
For honey for his queen at home.

Brown shall the man grow, being wooed
With the sun's kisses, brave and good,
Shall be an-hungered, and being fed,
Shall find his bed a golden bed.

Squirrels and hares and gamesome things,
And all sweet folk that go on wings,
Shall sit with him when he shall eat,
And ask a blessing on his meat.

The wonders of the skies for him
Shall open, nor his eyes be dim;
And seeing the first leaf unfold,
He shall praise God an hundredfold.

THE GARDENER

Yea, he shall learn from his employ
How God turns mourning into joy,
And from earth's graves calls up at last
His flowers when all the Winter's past.

SING, CUCKOO

Cuckoo calls in the heavenly weather

Cuckoo !

I, my Love, and the Spring together.

Soft are dreams of clear waters falling,

Cuckoo !

Softer yet is the Cuckoo calling.

Veils of distance cover and hide him,

Cuckoo !

Cuckoo comes and the Spring beside him.

Cuckoo utters the one call only,

Cuckoo !

Lacking Cuckoo the Spring were lonely.

THE LITTLE RED LARK

THE little red lark is shaking his wings,
Straight from the breast of his love he springs ;
Listen the lilt of the song he sings,
      All in the morning early, O.

The sea is rocking a cradle, hark !
To a hushing-song, and the fields are dark,
And would I were there with the little red lark,
      All in the morning early, O.

The beard of barley is old-man's-gray,
All green and silver the new-mown hay,
The dew from his wings he has shaken away,
      All in the morning early, O.

THE LITTLE RED LARK

The little red lark is high in the sky,
No eagle soars where the lark may fly.
Where are you going to, high, so high?
        All in the morning early, O.

His wings and feathers are sunrise red,
He hails the sun and his golden head:
Good-morrow, sun, you are long abed.
        All in the morning early, O.

I would I were where the little red lark
Up in the dawn like a rose-red spark,
Sheds the day on the fields so dark,
        All in the morning early, O.

VITA NUOVA

THE miracle of the new leaf
Tempers my joy, and stills my grief,
Renews my hope, my trust,
That late were bowed even to the dust.

I see in the young blades of grass
God's face as in a looking-glass,
And read His meanings plain
In the spring scents and the young grain.

Or by an amber woodland brook
I scan God's thought as in a book,
Since the late-frozen spring
Begins to leap, begins to sing.

O flower that only came to go,

Red as a rose and white as snow,

Will you not come again

After the winter and the rain?

SPRING LONGING

Often I wish that I might be
  This gay and golden weather
Among my father's fields, ah, me !
  And he and I together.

Below the mountains, fair and dim,
  My father's fields are spreading.
I 'd rather tread the sward with him
  Than I would dance at a wedding.

O green and fresh your English sod
  With daisies sprinkled over ;
But greener far were the fields I trod,
  And the honeyed Irish clover.

O, well your skylark cleaves the blue
  To bid the sun good-morrow ;
He has not the bonny song I knew
  High over an Irish furrow.

And often, often, I 'm longing still
  This gay and golden weather,
For my father's face by an Irish hill,
  And he and I together.

THE DAWNING OF THE DAY

As I roamed out one morning,
  The stars were in the sky ;
But Chanticleer his warning
  Had flung it low and high.
The little birds were talking,
  The mountains yet were gray,
When Colleen Dhas came walking
  At dawning of the day.

Her feet outvied the daisies,
  Her hair outshone the sun ;
Her beauty, like the Graces,
  Did join all sweets in one.

37

Her eyes like twin-stars married,
  Her breath of new-mown hay ;
A milking-pail she carried
  At dawning of the day.

Now, are you tender Hebe ?
  Or may be Juno bright ?
Your name it might be Phœbe,
  That robs the sun of light.
Or are you lovely Venus
  That close beside me stray ?
With the milking-pail between us
  At dawning of the day.

Young man, she said, don't flatter,
  Your glance is bold and free ;
No stranger's praise will matter
  To virtuous maids like me.

THE DAWNING OF THE DAY

Pray go where you were going,
  I take the other way ;
And I hear my Crummy lowing
  At dawning of the day.

Upon a bench of rushes
  Alone I sat and heard
Her voice outsing the thrushes
  And every wakening bird.
I heard the sweet milk spirting,
  The hedge between us lay,
And I longed that we were courting
  At dawning of the day.

SWEETS

SYRINGA and pink may,
        Roses,
And breath of new-mown hay.

Syringa and white may,
        Lilies,
The censer swings all day.

All night the censer fumes ;
        Moonlight
Heavy with dim perfumes.

Such sweets syringa shed,
        Honey,
That May when we were wed.

40

SWEETS

Such sweets syringa poured,
    Silver,
And love was prince and lord.

Syringa and sweet may,
    Roses,
Lilies, for Love's own day.

.

FAREWELL

Not soon shall I forget—a sheet
Of golden water, cold and sweet,
The young moon with her head in veils
Of silver, and the nightingales.

A wain of hay came up the lane—
O fields I shall not walk again,
And trees I shall not see, so still
Against a sky of daffodil !

Fields where my happy heart had rest,
And where my heart was heaviest,
I shall remember them at peace
Drenched in moon-silver like a fleece.

FAREWELL

The golden water sweet and cold,

The moon of silver and of gold,

The dew upon the grey grass-spears,

I shall remember them with tears.

CUCKOO

His voice runs before me ; I follow, it flies :
It is now in the meadow, and now 'mid the skies ;
So blithesome, so lightsome, now distant, now
    here,
And when he calls Cuckoo, the summer is near.

He calls back the roses, red roses that went
At the first blast of winter, so sad and forspent,
With the dew in their bosoms, young roses and
    dear,
And when he calls Cuckoo, the summer is near.

I would twine him a gold cage, but what would
    he do
For his world of the emerald, his bath in the blue,

CUCKOO

And his wee feathered comrades to make him
   good cheer?
And when he calls Cuckoo, the summer is near.

Now, blackbird, give over your harping of gold!
Brown thrush and green linnet, your music
   withhold!
The flutes of the forest are silver and clear,
But when he calls Cuckoo, the summer is here.

Good is an Orchard, the Saint saith,
To meditate on life and death,
With a cool well, a hive of bees,
A hermit's grot below the trees.

Good is an Orchard : very good,
Though one should wear no monkish hood
Right good, when Spring awakes her flute,
And good in yellowing time of fruit.

Very good in the grass to lie
And see the network 'gainst the sky,
A living lace of blue and green,
And boughs that let the gold between.

OF AN ORCHARD

The bees are types of souls that dwell
With honey in a quiet cell;
The ripe fruit figures goldenly
The soul's perfection in God's eye.

Prayer and praise in a country home,
Honey and fruit: a man might come,
Fed on such meats, to walk abroad,
And in his Orchard talk with God.

A LOST GARDEN

The cuckoo's note is nearly over,
  The jocund voice and dear,
I shall not hear him call, bright rover,
  Next year.

The little lilies, gold and sunny,
  And flecked with scarlet stain,
I shall not smell their musk and honey
  Again.

Gold roses in the garden growing,
  Red roses, damask, dear,
I shall not watch the roses blowing
  Next year.

48

A LOST GARDEN

I shall not hear the birds outpouring
   Love's rapture and its pain,
Nor see the singing lark and soaring,
      Again.

O garden of my dreams, keep ever
   My sacred dreams and dear,
But I shall come again, ah, never,
      Next year.

THE WOOD-DOVE

THE first sound that I hear at morn
In the low house where I was born
Is plaint of the wood-dove forlorn,
Leaning her breast upon a thorn.

All day in orchard coppices
The love-moan of the wood-dove is.
Song-birds all singing, give less bliss
Than she who mourns Love's little ease.

Crickets in sunny grass a-whir,
And many a bronze-winged trumpeter,
All the blithe country shine and stir,
And from all these I turn to her.

50

THE WOOD-DOVE

All noon, in the gold shade and sun,
Love's litany she doth intone,
Joining two lovers' names in one,
That shall not join till time be done.

All the gold afternoon again
She makes sweet music of her pain—
Love's captive, that yet hugs her chain
And of Love's whip and scourge is fain.

At night, when all the linnets keep
Silence, and bats and owlets creep,
Ere ever I fall to honeyed sleep,
I hear the wood-dove weep and weep.

DROUGHT

THE sky is greyer than doves,
Hardly a zephyr moves,
Little voices complain,
The leaves rustle before the rain.

No thrush is singing now,
All is still in the heart o' the bough ;
Only the trembling cry
Of young leaves murmuring thirstily.

Only the moan and stir
Of little hands in the boughs I hear,
Beckoning the rain to come
Out of the evening, out of the gloom.

DROUGHT

The wind's wings are still,
Nothing stirs but the singing rill
And hearts that complain.
The leaves rustle before the rain.

THE PRETTY GIRL MILKING HER COW

(Colleen dhas Cruidthe-na-mo)

THE dewdrops were grey on the clover,
   The grey mists of night were withdrawn,
The blackbird sang clear from the cover,
   The hills wore the rose of the dawn.
But sweeter than blackbirds and thrushes,
   Her song, whom the Graces endow,
And pinker than dawn her soft blushes,
   The pretty girl milking her cow.

She sang, and the milk, sweet and scented,
   Spirted white as the breast of my dear.
She sang, and the cow, grown contented,
   Gave over her kicking to hear.

THE PRETTY GIRL MILKING HER COW

O wildest of little black Kerries,
    You will come at her call, I know how,
Since my heart at her voice leaps and scurries,
    The pretty girl milking her cow.

As she sang I drew nearer each minute,
    A captive in Love's rosy chain,
And my heart every second was in it
    Grew fuller of joy and of pain,
Till I cried out behind her: My storeen,
    Pray guess who is holding you now?
And I felt the heart-beats of my Noreen,
    The pretty girl milking her cow.

I kissed her sweet eyelids to blind her,
    I kissed her black head like the silk,
The cow—who was going to bind her?—
    With one kick kicked over the milk.

And then, growing bolder and bolder,
   I kissed from the chin to the brow ;
She was mine ere the day was much older,
   The pretty girl milking her cow.

THE WIND THAT SHAKES THE BARLEY

THERE's music in my heart all day,
  I hear it late and early,
It comes from fields are far away,
  The wind that shakes the barley.
     Ochone !

Above the uplands drenched with dew,
  The sky hangs soft and pearly,
An emerald world is listening to
  The wind that shakes the barley.
     Ochone !

57

Above the bluest mountain crest
    The lark is singing rarely,
It rocks the singer into rest,
    The wind that shakes the barley.
        Ochone !

Oh, still through summers and through springs
    It calls me late and early.
Come home, come home, come home, it sings,
    The wind that shakes the barley.
        Ochone !

THE GREEN FIELDS TO AMERICA

THE green fields to America make my heart sore,

The green fields to America that I have travelled
o'er;

Oh, many and many a mile they stretch so wide
and free,

The green fields to America betwixt my love
and me!

There's a pretty bird, a birdeen grey, he swings
on high,

Nor fears at all the pathless main, the trackless
sky;

Oh, if I had that birdeen's wings, 'tis I would take
The green fields from America, for my love's sake.

Oh, what to me were wastes of storm and miles
of sea,
The compass in my heart points straight to my
countree,
To where my love sits quietly beside the sands
Of the green fields to America with his head in
his hands.

The little fields we once did roam were gold and
green,
And here are but the washing waves and white
foam between ;
Above the little fields at home the hills are blue :
God bless the kindly fields at home, the fond
love I knew.

THE GREEN FIELDS TO AMERICA

Now God and Mary strengthen me to take that
way,

The green fields from America some lucky day,

And God and Mary bring me safe, to stray no
more

From the little fields I knew of old and kind love
of yore !

MUSHROOMS

These be the mushroom days, and lo !
The mushroom rings so darkly grow,
Round as a wedding-ring, and set
With pearls as sweet as violet.

Who made the rings so fine and round
Twined in and out by hollow and mound ?
And who hath summoned mushrooms hither,
Here where the fairies dance together ?

Here are the tracks of feet that went
Before the day, in dew and scent,
Before the dew was dried, and trod
The mushroom-strewn and emerald sod.

MUSHROOMS

Who were the early risers who
That in the grey dusk and the dew
Brushed with their cloaks the gossamer,
And set the shivering grass astir?

The owl his counsel well doth keep,
The wood-dove she was fast asleep,
The lark was up too late to see
The mushrooms gather on hill and lea.

The earth-bound corncrake, she might know,
But that she went a month ago
To Egypt, where she lieth hid
Sand-deep beside a pyramid,

Nursing her honey-voice; well then
The mystery, mystery must remain—
Since eyes of birds nor human eyes
No fairy secret shall surprise—

MUSHROOMS

Of who in dew and dawn did fashion

The fairy rings in sweet rotation,

And set the mushrooms in the ring,

And who came hither mushrooming.

POPLAR

THE blinding sky's unkind,
  The day has dust and glare,
The poplar keeps the wind
  In her cage of light and air,
Makes of her leaves a snare
  To keep the wind confined ;
All in the breathless glare
  The poplar holds the wind.

O cool and beautiful
  Her leaves of silver-gray
Hang in the wind so cool
  In the blind and breathless day '

POPLAR

Turn in the wind at play,
  Fresh as a little pool
That in the forest gray
  Holds silver fins and cool.

All other trees are still,
  The oak, the elm, and the beech,
But the poplar hath her fill
  Of soft and gracious speech.
The winds are out of reach
  Beyond the sea and the hill
For the oak, and elm, and beech,
  But the poplar hath her fill.

THE GREY MORNINGS

THE grey mornings I well remember,
The grey mountains new-waked from slumber,
The grey dews on the trees and hedges,
And in grey distance the grey sea's edges.

Cool it was, sweet beyond telling,
The grey-green hay in the pastures smelling,
The grey meadows wet as a river,
The grey dew where the grass-blades quiver.

Grey gulls and the sea-grey swallow
Take the track that my heart would follow,
Home from the heat and the cruel weather,
That I and my heart might fare together!

THE GREY MORNINGS

Purple-grey are the wild hills showing,
Silver-grey is the west wind blowing.
O grey fields and grey hills behind you,
Would my feet might follow and find you !

APPLES

ALL day in a green bower I sit,
Ripe apples drop about my feet,
Ripe apples drop about my head,
And in my very lap are shed.

Hither is blown no city chime,
The falling apples mark the time,
For every minute one falls down.
Thud ! there's another minute flown.

The rosy, smiling, sunburnt faces,
They have their bed in the sweet grasses,
Like children's heads that sisterly
Upon the same soft pillow lie.

APPLES

Here are Heartsease and Honesty,
And Honeysuckle for the bee,
And Love-in-Idleness to stand
And keep the gates on either hand.

The air is rich with apple-scent,
Yet since no mortal lot's content,
The apple-loving wasp is given
To trouble my terrestrial heaven.

THE FOGGY DEW

A SPLENDID place is London, with golden store
For them that have the heart and hope and
    youth galore ;
But mournful are its streets to me, I tell you
    true,
For I 'm longing sore for Ireland in the foggy
    dew.

The sun he shines all day here, so fierce and fine,
With never a wisp of mist at all to dim his shine ;
The sun he shines all day here from skies of blue,
He hides his face in Ireland in the foggy dew.

The maids go out to milking in the pastures gray,
The sky is green and golden at dawn of the day ;

And in the deep-drenched meadows the hay lies
new,

And the corn is turning yellow in the foggy dew.

Mavrone! if I might feel now the dew on my
face,

And the wind from the mountains in that re-
membered place,

I'd give the wealth of London, if mine it were
to do,

And I'd travel home to Ireland and the foggy
dew.

THE RED DEER

(AT KILLARNEY)

THERE are lords of the forest,
 And lords of the glen,
And lords of the waters,
 And lords over men.
The birds of the blue air,
 The fish of the mere,
All, all have their masters
 Except the red deer.

From the heights of the mountain
 Where no man shall tread,
Where in furze and in bracken
 The deer hath his bed,

He will swim the fair waters,
From heaven to heaven,
He is this man's at morning,
And that man's at even.

No! free as the west wind
That comes from the ocean
And tosses the bright woods
And waves to commotion,—
No! free as the stars are,
The sun's not more free:
He is free as the waters
Escaped to the sea.

Ah, ye who would claim him,
Be silent at last,
Ye are gone like the bright leaves
Blown high on the blast.

THE RED DEER

With your castles and abbeys,
  Through time he remaineth
The red deer of freedom
  Whom no man enchaineth.

AN ANTHEM IN HEAT

Now praise the Lord, both moon and sun,
    And praise Him, all ye nights and days,
And golden harvests every one,
    And all ye hidden waterways,
With cattle standing to the knees
    Safe from the bitter gadfly's sting ;
But praise Him most, O little breeze
    That walks abroad at evening.

O praise Him, all ye orchards now,
    And all ye gardens deep in green,
Ripe apples on the yellowing bough,
    And golden plum and nectarine,

AN ANTHEM IN HEAT

And peaches ruddier than the rose,
    And pears against the southern wall;
But most the little wind that blows,
    The blessed wind at evenfall.

O praise Him, hoary dews again,
    Drenching the meadows 'neath the moon,
And praise Him hidden founts of rain,
    And amber brooks singing a tune,
And icy deeps of well-water,
    And each pellucid stream and spring;
But praise Him most, O wind astir,
    O blessed wind at evening.

O praise Him now, ye burning days
    Of golden summer, hot and spent;
Planets and stars, see that His praise
    Be blown about the firmament.

Yet praise Him best, O little wind
    That out of heaven will blow and call,
Because, because our God is kind
    And bids us live at evenfall.

SPARROW

When August hangs the bough with plums,
The dusty city sparrow comes
For sojourn in the country sweet,
To taste the barley and the wheat.

Like any country bird he walks
Down the gold aisles of bearded stalks,
Pecks juicy grains in ear, and takes
His pleasure in the barley-brakes.

He bathes in dew at morn, and preens
His sooty coat to mock the sheens
Of swallow, fieldfare, finch, and wren
That hate the dusty ways of men.

79

SPARROW

His cynic wit, his mocking eye,
The innocent country ways decry;
Though dews may wash his feathers clean
He hath the urchin's heart within.

The gossip his of chimney-stacks,
Wherefore the pleasant country lacks
Something, his ear the silence tires
Who nests amid the city spires.

To the perpetual green and gold
In dusk and dew his eyes are cold;
For his untravelled heart yet turns
Home where the smoky city burns.

A little while for health he stays
Where Flora paints the country ways,
But holds that still the town is best
For men and birds of wit and taste.

OF THE APPLE

The apples in the garden bed,
  Turned ripe and rosy to the south,
The youngest novice shook her head,
  And eyed them with a watering mouth.

She said : 'Our Mother Eve wrought woe
  Once with the deadly apple's bite,
God keep mine eyes from following so
  After my evil appetite.'

Down came the saint, and gathered then
  Of all the ripest, sweetest one,
Clear amber-cheeked, with ruddy stain,
  From the hot kisses of the sun.

She ate, and praised God as she ate,
 That He made apples very good.
' He might,' she said, ' have given the date,
 The fig, the orange, for our food ;

' Nor yet made apples, to delight
 The eye, the smell, the palate fine :
For these my grateful appetite
 Praises the Giver kind, divine.

' Sister,' she said : ' Come, pluck and eat,
 And thank with me the Lord, who made
For us such flavours, cool and sweet ;
 Wherewith the world abounds,' she said.

MANY WATERS

There were live waters racing down,
    The air was full of exquisite sound,
Rainbows of spray wove them a crown,
    For pools wherein the sun lay drowned.

Streams from the heights of Mangerton,
    And from the crest of Torc, sweet streams,
Golden and brown, came singing on :
    I hear the music in my dreams.

Drip, drip, from every rock there fell
    A fringe of golden water fine,
Sweet as dew in the lily-bell,
    Golden as honey, clear as wine.

The streams ran in the roads, the streams
  Danced through the bracken and the fern,
Played hide-and-seek till there were gleams
  Of gold water at every turn.

The mountains they were still in the sky,
  The red deer never stirred in the woods,
The eagle kept his eyrie high :
  These were the loveliest solitudes.

The roar of the Torc Waterfall
  Was dreamy, all the lakes lay still ;
There was no bird singing at all :
  My heart of music had her fill.

AUTUMN DAY

THE day goeth in gray
    Like a gray nun ;
There's a bird on the highest spray
    Singing that summer's done :
Singing so sad and gay
    Of summers over and gone.

The day's wimple of gray
    Round her cheeks drawn
Hides what her eyes say ;
    A wimple finer than lawn
Hides the eyes of the day
    Since the gray flower of dawn.

AUTUMN DAY

She counteth her rosaries
   Of the minutes and hours.
Dewy gray are her eyes—
   Gray eyes, sweeter than flowers.
She keepeth her mysteries
   Holy in her gray bowers.

The day goeth so slow,
   Like a gray nun,
Whispering sweet and low
   Orison, benison.
And only to see her go
   The stars come one by one.

THE TREE'S DOUBLE

How beautiful the tree-shadows lie on
 The paler green o' the grasses !
 October wind stirs them a little and passes,
Cloud-shadows sail above them and are gone.

The trees are like a golden fountain's spray,
 Like golden waters raining.
 When the October skies and ways are waning,
The trees alone have the heart to be gay.

Yet there's a blue sky, and the sun is gold,
 A gold tree and a bird in it,
 A Jenny Wren or a belated linnet,
Singing away though all the nests are cold.

THE TREE'S DOUBLE

The tree upon the grass has a bird's shadow,
  As the live tree its bird,
  Shadow and substance joyfully praise the Lord
As well as when the world was all a meadow.

And when the living tree rocks at its pleasure
  Its bird in frolic glee,
  The shadow-bird within the shadow-tree
Dances upon the grass to the same measure.

LOVE LIES BLEEDING

In my heart's else barren ground
    Love-lies-bleeding,
Love lies all one bitter wound.

Heart's-ease, she is done and over;
    Roses, lilies,
Drifted leaves of autumn cover.

Ah, poor Love, so full of blisses,
    And so lately
Love-in-a-mist of love and kisses.

89

LOVE LIES BLEEDING

Ah, poor Love, who built so high !
   Who shall build us
Nests whence never a bird shall fly ?

In my heart's plot, winter-gray,
   Love-lies-bleeding
For the bird that's flown away.

AUTUMN

THE things the Autumn took away
　　With no returning Spring shall come,
Never with leaf upon the spray,
　　Never with bud nor bloom,
Nor lambs that make high holiday.

April will come again and May,
　　And the green world forget her gloom,
And roses in the garden gray
　　Yield up their full perfume;
And blackbirds sing the livelong day.

O dancing leaves and winds at play,
　　For Spring shall bring the swallows home,
And nightingales and scent of hay.
　　But there shall never come
That which the Autumn took away.

FLOOD

Across the vale the floods are out,
The floods are out with rush and rout,
Across the world the floods are out,
    The land is in the sea.
And round the oak-tree that displays
The bronze-bright head in wintry days,
The roaring current swings and sways,
    Shouting his song of glee.

And landsmen now are watermen,
The robin as the water-hen,
That makes her nest in reed and fen,
    The robin's gone afloat.

FLOOD

The wind that rocks him to and fro
With a soft cradle-song and slow,
Pleases him in the ebb and flow,
    Rocking him in a boat.

Flotsam and jetsam whirling by
The bridge where lovers meet and sigh,
The whirling crows flap wings and cry,
    And praise themselves that they
Have built their homes, one story each,
In the tall masts of elm and beech,
And them no swelling flood can reach
    Till all the world be grey.

NOVEMBER

GREEN and gold and gold and gray,
Willows by the waterway
Shake their gray-green locks and shiver
At their faces in the river.

But the emerald fields and bright
Sleep out in the rain all night;
And all day the rain and shine
Swell the emerald veins like wine.

Gold and gray and green and gold,
Every spreading oak behold;
Like the rosy, burning bush
Whence God spoke 'mid awe and hush.

NOVEMBER

Green and gold and gold and gray,

Sunset smiles from far away,

Palest gold, and gray clouds cover

The pale golden head all over.

CRUEL WINTER

The dear song-thrush is dead,
The valley hath instead
  Only the silence.
The silence aches all day
In hills and valleys gray,
  Islands and highlands.

Song-thrush, asthore, where went
Your singing-voice unspent,
  Into what shadows?
What vales of honey dew
Listen and long with you,
  What woods, what meadows?

CRUEL WINTER

O Spring that came so late,
O Winter desolate,
   Lingering, doleful!
The dear song-thrush that's cold
In lands of summer gold
   Singeth his soul full.

MODEREEN RUE

(*i.e.* THE LITTLE RED ROGUE—THE FOX)

OCH, Modereen Rue, you little red rover,
By the glint of the moon you stole out of your
cover,
And now there is never an egg to be got,
Nor a handsome fat chicken to put in the pot.
Och, Modereen Rue!

With your nose to the earth and your ear on the
listen,
You slunk through the stubble with frost-drops
a-glisten,

With my lovely fat drake in your teeth as you
went,

That your red roguish children should breakfast
content.

Och, Modereen Rue!

Och, Modereen Rue, hear the horn for a warning,

They are looking for red roguish foxes this
morning;

But let them come my way, you little red
rogue,

'Tis I will betray you to huntsman and dog.

Och, Modereen Rue!

The little red rogue, he's the colour of bracken,

O'er mountains, o'er valleys, his pace will not
slacken.

Tantara! tantara! he is off now, and, faith!

'Tis a race 'twixt the little red rogue and his
  death.

Och, Modereen Rue!

Och, Modereen Rue, I 've no cause to be grieving

For little red rogues with their tricks and their
  thieving.

The hounds they give tongue, and the quarry's
  in sight,

The hens on the roost may sleep easy to-night.

Och, Modereen Rue!

But my blessing be on him. He made the
  hounds follow

Through the woods, through the dales, over hill,
  over hollow,

MODEREEN RUE

It was Modereen Rue led them fast, led them
   far,
From the glint of the morning till eve's silver
   star.

       Och, Modereen Rue!

And he saved his red brush for his own future
   wearing,
He slipped into a drain, and he left the hounds
   swearing.
Good luck, my fine fellow, and long may you
   show
Such a clean pair of heels to the hounds as
   they go.

       Och, Modereen Rue!

THE CHRISTMAS BIRD

BELOW the stable eaves that saw
The blessed Baby laid in straw,
A little wren had built her nest.
She, honoured as the harmless beast,
Beheld the holy Birth with awe.

Sweet, sweet! she sang, and still *Sweet, sweet!*
O sweetest Babe from head to feet!
And sweet, sweet Mother!   To and fro
She fluttered; her small heart aglow
Enraptured her with holy heat.

O happy I! she said, *who stayed*
When every Jenny Wren, afraid

THE CHRISTMAS BIRD

At the first frost, fled to the South.
I would I had the blackbird's mouth
To praise this Babe and Mother-Maid!

I would I might strip off, she said,
Gold feathers from my breast and head,
Enough to warm and shield withal
This comfortless small Babe in stall,
And would my feathers were His bed!

Then by the manger perched that bird
With *Gloria, gloria* to the Lord!
Who would have thought so small a throat
Had room for such a piercing note?
The singing stars and angels heard.

Therefore they call the little wren
Ever the Blessèd Mary's hen.

Therefore no boy shall cast a stone
When Jenny Wren, sitting her lone,
Sings how God came on earth for men.

Therefore her eggs be safe in tree
And all her merry brood go free.

Acknowledgments to the *Pall Mall Gazette*, which sheltered, when new-born, some forty of these fledglings. Also to the *New Review*, the *Westminster Gazette*, the *Illustrated London News*, and the Chicago *Chap-Book*.